Copyright © 1998 by Nord-Süd Verlag AG, Gossau Zürich, Switzerland.
First published in Switzerland under the title *Stadtmaus und Landmaus.*

All rights reserved.
No part of this book may be reproduced or utilized in any form
or by any means, electronic or mechanical, including photocopying,
recording, or any information storage and retrieval system,
without permission in writing from the publisher.

First published in the United States, Great Britain, Canada,
Australia, and New Zealand in 1998 by North-South Books,
an imprint of Nord-Süd Verlag AG, Gossau Zürich, Switzerland.

Distributed in the United States by North-South Books Inc., New York.

Library of Congress Cataloging-in-Publication Data
Watts, Bernadette.
[Stadtmaus un Landmaus. English]
The town mouse and the country mouse : an Aesop
fable / retold & illustrated by Bernadette Watts.
First published in Switzerland under the title:
Stadtmaus und Landmaus.
Summary: When the town mouse and the country mouse
visit each other, they find they prefer very different ways of life.
ISBN 1-55858-987-2 (trade)—ISBN 1-55858-988-0 (library)
[1. Fables. 2. Mice—Folklore.] I. Aesop. II. Country mouse
and the city mouse. III. Title.
PZ8.2.W35To   1998
398.24′529353—dc21   98-6472

A CIP catalogue record for this book is available from The British Library.
ISBN 1-55858-987-2 (trade binding)
3 5 7 9 TB 10 8 6 4 2
ISBN 1-55858-988-0 (library binding)
1 3 5 7 9 LB 10 8 6 4 2
Printed in Belgium

For more information about our books, and the authors and artists
who create them, visit our web site: www.northsouth.com

THE TOWN MOUSE
AND THE COUNTRY MOUSE
~ An Aesop Fable ~

RETOLD & ILLUSTRATED BY

Bernadette Watts

NORTH~SOUTH BOOKS

NEW YORK · LONDON

Every evening the country mouse
climbed out of her house into the meadow.
She loved to feel the last sunbeams of the
day warming her fur.

One evening she looked across the
meadow to the town. "I wonder what the
city mice eat," she said to herself. "Where
do they find seeds and berries? I think
I'll go there and have a look."

She packed some tasty treats in her
basket and tripped across the fields to
the town.

The country mouse went hesitantly into the town. The tall buildings rearing up on both sides looked sinister to her. She scurried nervously from one building to the next. Soon her feet hurt from walking on the hard ground. "Perhaps I should turn back," she murmured to herself. "I don't see anyone—"

"Psst!" someone whispered.
The country mouse turned and saw a town mouse looking out from a crack in a wall.
"I come from—"
"You come right in here! Quick!" cried the town mouse. "It's dangerous out there!" She scurried off, and the country mouse ran after her.

The two mice crawled down a long passage.
In her haste, the country mouse hit her head
on something hard, and got such a shock that
she dropped her basket.

"Oh!" she squeaked. "Those are the tasty treats I brought with me. Wait! I've got to pick them up."

"I'll help you," said the town mouse. "But you don't need them. I'd like you to be my guest."

At last they came to a hole in an old wooden panel.

"Here we are. Come and look!" said the town mouse proudly.

The country mouse hesitated. There was a strange smell. But finally curiosity overcame her and she looked inside. She was amazed by what she saw!

There was a room, much bigger than anything the country mouse had ever seen. Bigger than a fox's hole. Even bigger than a badger's den. Everywhere she looked there were unfamiliar things.

"Try some. It's delicious!" said the town mouse, pointing at a piece of cheese.

The country mouse liked the taste of the cheese, but she ate so much it gave her a stomachache.

"Drink some of this tea," said the town mouse. "Then you can lie down over there."

The country mouse watched the mice happily scampering about. She began to feel sleepy. Half-awake, she dreamed of her little house and all her familiar things. At last her eyes closed.

The next morning she was the first to get up.

"Dear town mouse," said the country mouse. "Thank you for everything. You have been very kind to me, but I want to go home now."

The town mouse led her out to the street, and they said good-bye to each other.

The country mouse ran out of the town as fast as she could. How lovely it was to run over soft ground again, to feel the sun's warmth on her fur, and to breathe in the scent of the meadow!

She sat in her armchair in her snug little home, exhausted but contented.

A few days later she heard someone calling
from the field:

"Country mouse, where are you?"

"It's the town mouse!" thought the country
mouse as she climbed out of her house.

"How nice that you've come to visit me," she said.

"I wanted to see how you live," the town mouse replied, "but the journey here was terrible! My feet hurt!"

"Come and cool them in the dew," said the country mouse.

"Here, step into this pool of dew," said the country mouse kindly. "It will soothe the pain."

The town mouse soon recovered.

"I've brought some cheese for you," she said with a smile.

"Thank you. That was very kind. But you must try some good country food while you are here," the country mouse replied.

The country mouse led the town mouse into her home.

"Here is where I live. Please make yourself comfortable," she said.

The town mouse snuffled around inquisitively. She found the smell of damp earth strange. How small everything was here! And yet quite comfortable, somehow.

The country mouse offered the town mouse
a hazelnut.
　　The town mouse nibbled at it cautiously.
It was good.

The country mouse led the town mouse into her larder.

"Try these, dear friend. They are some of the very best things I have," she said, pointing to a basket of berries.

The town mouse bit into a berry. "Mmm, wonderfully sweet," she said. "You have a good life here. But still, I prefer my own home."

The town mouse and the country mouse looked at each other for a long time.

Then the town mouse said, "Thank you for everything. May I come and visit you again?"

"Oh yes, do!" replied the country mouse cheerfully. "And please bring more of that cheese. I really like it."

As the moon rose, the country mouse accompanied the town mouse a little way across the meadow.

They hugged good-bye.

"We'll see each other again soon!" they promised.

Then each went her own way, back to the home she loved.